For Melissa—a sister and a friend —ML

For Chester and Mya —CJ

Carolrhoda Books
A division of Lerner Publishing Group, Inc.
241 First Avenue North
Minneapolis, MN 55401 USA

For reading levels and more information, look up this title at www.lernerbooks.com.

Designed by Emily Harris.
Main body text set in Bawdy 18/22. Typeface provided by Chank.
The illustrations in this book were created digitally using various paintbrushes in Adobe Photoshop. The hardware used included a Cintiq drawing tablet and an iMac computer.

Library of Congress Cataloging-in-Publication Data

Names: Lee, Mark, 1950– author. | Jevons, Chris illustrator.
Title: My best friend is a goldfish / by Mark Lee ; illustrated by Chris Jevons.
Description: Minneapolis, MN : Carolrhoda Books, [2017] | Summary: When a boy and his best friend storm off after an argument, the boy searches for a new best friend.
Identifiers: LCCN 2016008151 (print) | LCCN 2016033716 (ebook) | ISBN 9781512426014 (lb : alk. paper) | ISBN 9781512430011 (eb pdf)
Subjects: | CYAC: Best friends—Fiction. | Friendship—Fiction.
Classification: LCC PZ7.L51394 My 2017 (print) | LCC PZ7.L51394 (ebook) | DDC [E]—dc23

LC record available at https://lccn.loc.gov/2016008151

Manufactured in the United States of America
1-41366-23310-6/7/2017

MY BEST FRIEND
IS A
GOLDFISH

Mark Lee

illustrated by Chris Jevons

Carolrhoda Books • Minneapolis

If you ask me, a best friend is the best thing in the world.

Best friends enjoy the same things.

They play together all the time.

And they *always* get along with each other.

That is why . . .

My best friend is Murphy, my dog.
Murphy howls when he hears a police siren. This is FUN!

Murphy likes to sniff everything. Me too!

And you can eat really fast when your food is in a bowl on the floor.

We love taking walks in the park . . .

But that's where Murphy plays with his REAL friends.

My best friend is ~~Murphy, my dog.~~
Gus, my cat.

We like to nap on the couch together.
Gus is teaching me how to purr.

We sneak around the house together . . .

and pounce!

My best friend is ~~Murphy, my dog.~~
~~Gus, my cat.~~
Hercules, my hamster.

Hercules doesn't have pockets, so he stores food in his cheeks.

I don't have hamster cheeks. And that is why . . .

My best friend is ~~Murphy, my dog.~~
~~Gus, my cat.~~
~~Hercules, my hamster.~~
Fishy Robert, my goldfish.

It's quiet underwater. We both like to float and look out at the world.

We don't need forks or spoons.
We nibble on flakes of food.

Fishy Robert eats.

Then he swims around.

Then he eats.

Then he swims around—

My best friend is ~~Murphy, my dog.~~
~~Gus, my cat.~~
~~Hercules, my hamster.~~
~~Fishy Robert, my goldfish.~~

There's this kid I knew who moved to Brazil.

What about . . . Captain Blastoff, the Space Pirate!

Mr. Teddy?

I really like my friends, but they aren't always like me.

Then again, cookies and milk are different . . .

. . . and they're still perfect for each other.

My best friend is—

"Hey! You know what you are?"

"What?"

"You're it!"